CONTENTS

1. Basic Meaning of Sales & Marketing.
2. Categories of Sales.
3. What a Sales Person Sales (Product).
4. What is a Product?
5. What are the types of Products?

A. Consumer product.
B. Technical product.

1. What is consumer product?
2. What is Technical product?
3. What are the Sales Steps required for Selling a product
4. Detailed Explanation of Sales Step through (ODPEC) with Case Studied.
5. Definition of Customer.
6. Types of Customers.
7. Basic Meaning of Company.
8. Structural Function of Company, Products from Company to Consumer.
9. Terms we use in Sales.
10. How to appoint a new distributor.
11. What are the Schemes & how to calculate the Scheme?
12. What is the meaning of retailor & wholesaler?
13. How to calculate return on investment (ROI).
14. What is the Company Hierarchy
15. What Sales Person does before going to the market place for selling a product?
16. How to use different type sales dairy Technical or non-Technical.
17. Personality development.

18. Paper required for the monthly review meeting
19. How to learn the language of sales
20. How to be a good personality of Sales.
21. Case Study.

1. Basic Meaning of Sales & Marketing

Marketing is the macro concept which includes.

a. Sales
b. Banking
c. Finance
d. Insurance
e. Adverting

But here we want to become the sales professional so we have to study only about the sales.

SALES. The basic meaning of sales is the exchange of goods in term of money for earning profit is called sales.

2. Categories of sales

Sales are Categorise in two parts.

a. Direct Sales
b. Indirect Sales

DIRECT SALES. Direct sales means goods are sold to the direct user/consumer.e.g like vegetable seller; we have seen some gentlemen selling electronic goods door to door. This we call direct sale.

MAKE YOURSELF CAPABLE OF SALES & MARKETING

HOW TO QUALIFY YOURSELF IN SALES & MARKETING

KAMAL KANT

Copyright © Kamal Kant
All Rights Reserved.

INDIRECT SALE. Indirect sales men's the goods doesn't sale directly to the user rather it goes through different channels of distribution.

Question arises what are the channels of distribution.

CHANELS OF DISTRIBUTION.

a. FACTORY
b. Depot/warehouse
c. Super stockist
d. Distributors /Stockiest
e. Retailor /wholesaler
f. Users/consumers

FACTORY. Factory is defined as where the goods are manufactured for the use of consumers.

DEPOT/WAREHOUSE. Depot or warehouse is the place where the factory goods are stoked in bulk quantity for supply to next channel for distribution, the person who runs the operation of the depot is called the carrying & forwarding agents (C&F)

SUPER STOCKIST. Super stockist is the part of distribution that purchases goods from the C&F & supply to the distribution.

DISTRIBUTORS/STOCKIST. Distributor is that part of distribution channel that purchase goods from the super stockist & supply to the retailers /wholesalers

USERS/CONSUMERS. Users/Consumers directly purchase goods

3. What a Sales Person Sales (Products)

A Sales Person requiresthe given information

a. Basic knowledge about the product.
b. If the products are electronic the he should have the technical knowledge about the product.
c. He should have the knowledge how to demonstrate the product in working style.
d. If he is selling the food products he should have the knowledge about the ingredients available in the product & how they are beneficial for the health
e. He should have the knowledge about MRP/Price /Margin

4. What is a product?

What a sales person sales. A sales person sale anything that

We call it a product.

5. What are types of products?

Two types of products.

a. Consumer products
b. Technical products
c. **Consumer products.** Consumergoods are those which satisfy the consumer needs after direct use. Selling those

Goods the sales person should have the knowledge about

The basic ingredients of the products MRP rate and margin.

7. **Technical products.** For selling these products the sales person requires the technical knowledge for selling these products e.g. mobile car bikes, electronic machines etc.

8. **What are the sales step required for the selling a products**

Full knowledge required for selling a products, basic/technical

Source/ingredients MRP margin scheme distributor margin and

Retail margin etc. required for selling a products.

9. **Detailed Explanation of sales step through (ODPEC) with**

Case studies.

How the sales person dose sales, what are steps required while

Selling a products

O-opening the call

D-Developing the Call

P-Proposing

E-Eliminating the doubts

C-Closing

Opening the Calls-When the sales person visit to a retailor/

Distributor the following step to follow

a.   Wishing (good morning,Namaste,Hello)

b.   Your name from which company you are.

Developing call-In this step the sales person should develop

The platform between the buyer & seller (relation building &

Personal bounding) e.g. whether, politics, local issues, so that

You can build a good relationship with him.

Proposing-In the third step of selling the sales person should

Propose about the product what he is selling.

1. Product's introduction

2. Products Range Show

3. Rates & Scheme

Eliminating the doubts-This is very important step of selling

In this step of selling the sales person should clear all the

Doubts/questions of the buyer (about product wait/ net rate

QPS objection/profits/specialty of products what you sale)

If he is selling technical products he should clear about

Service places & how much time it will take to get repair or

Replace.

Closing- In the last step of selling is order taking. The sales

Person should take maximum order as much as possible, the

Call should be closed in win win situation. Take maximum

Order QTY (the buyer & seller should be happy)

10.   **Definition of Customer.** Any people who consume our product for satisfying his need or requirement is called the consumer.
11.   **Types** of customer.
12.   Customers are classified in different categories.
13.   Calculative Customer
14.   Egoistic Customer
15.   Talkative Customer
16.   Technical Customer
17.   Loyal Customer
18.   Educated Customer
19.   Negligent Customer

Calculative Customer- this type of customer are very calculative & profit conscious, so as a sales person you should be very alert & strong in data figures while doing the call.

Egoistic Customer- These customers are very conscious about their respect, reputation, image, good will, so as a sales person you should pay proper respect boost-up his ego, goodwill and image

Loyal Customer- This type of customer is very honest & loyal, so as a sales person you should be straight forward with this type of customer.

Talkative Customer- This type of costumer is talkative and interested worthless discussion, so the sales person should be alert not to involve in worthless discussion, you should hold is discussion and come on motive.

Technical Customer- This type of customer are knowledgeable technically about the product. So as a sales person you should have the proper technically knowledge about the product. If some micro technically is out of knowledge then the sales person should say I don't have any idea about it.it I will discuss with my specialist.

Educated Customer- This type of customer is educated and the sales person should do a call with limited discussion. You should answer only the asked question

Negligent Customer- This type of customer are negligent so the sales person should be very alert while taking order, he should check all the stocks properly in his shop while taking order of his product.(no pressure sale)

<u>For handling these type of customer we have to do case study though mock calls</u>.

13. Basic meaning of company/industries

A company is a association of person in which the group of people invest their capital for starting their business for earning profit, but an industry is a group of company that involve in one or more business.

14. Structural Function of a company's product from company to the

consumer.

What are the stage though which the product reaches from company to consumers?

COMPANY/INDUSTRY

DEPOT/WAREHOUSE

SUPERSTOCKIST

DISTRIBUTOR

RETAILOR/WHOLESELLER

CONSUMERS

15. Terms we are using in sales.

a. Call-visiting shop for taking order
b. TC-total call-how many shop sales person visit
c. PC/EC Productive Calls/Effective Calls-no of shop given order
d. Outlet /Counter-every shop we call the outlet/counter
e. Throughput/average-Average no of product we are given.
f. Beat-50-60 outlet in market we call it as beat.
g. Rout-rout can be cleared through mock call
h. Frequency-sales person covering the beat, it might be weekly forth nightly (after 15 days and monthly
a. DB(Distributor)
j. Primary Sales-billed to direct company /super
k. Secondary Sales-you sold the goods in the market
ax. SKU (Stock Keeping Unit)

all. 4P(Product Price Place Promotion)
n. AIDA(awareness interest desire action)
o. ABC (Always be Closing)
p. ABM (account based marketing)
q. ABS (account base Selling)
r. APS (average selling Price)
s. CRM (customer relationship management)
t.

u. **How to appoint a new distributor.**

For appointment of new distributor in the town we have to go through the follow steps.

a. The sales person has to do the wholesale market survey at least 25 shops and ask question about their service, behaviour and availability of stocks at distributor.
b. We have to do the retail survey at least 30 -35 shops their visit frequency and service
c. After doing the survey we have to prepare the territorial rank of the distributor.

<u>Question which we have to ask the retailor /wholesaler while doing the market survey</u>

a. How many distributor come on your shop, (write their name and phone number)
b. Which is the best among all(best men's timely service, good behaviour and proper scheme he is given)

<u>After doing the market survey we have to meet the shortlisted distributor. Now what question you have to ask to the distributor</u>

a. Self intro and Company intro

b. How many companies you are having distribution & which beats you are covering.

c. How many sales staff you are having for order booking , how many vehicles you are having for market supply.

d. How many outlets you are covering in the town.

e. How many credit you are given in the market

f. You have to ask the question regarding company wise turnover.

Question for your company

Are you interested to expend your business, because we are planning to appoint new distributor in your town.

If already having the beggar distributor in this town then the

Distributor will ask why you are changing the present distributor, disclose what actual problems you are facing the present distributor

With this discussion you have share your term & condition of the company.

a. Distributor margin (percentage of profit)

b. Schemes (primary/secondary)

c. Distributor claims process (Days for clearance of claims)

d. Damage /Expiry policy

e. Investment (days)

f. Present sale

If distributor is ready all condition, immediately fill the appointment form.

<u>Note-while doing survey and appointing the distributor, you have to write every think in your dairy.</u>

17. What are the scheme & how to calculate the scheme?

<u>Schemes are categories in two types.</u>

a. Primary scheme

b.Secondary scheme

Primary scheme-Primary scheme is that extra benefit to the distributor which deducted in the invoice or bill at the time or billing

Secondary scheme- Secondary scheme is that benefit to the distributor which the distributor gives to the retailer in the market. After in the company person makes the claim & company issue the credit note in the distributor.

<u>Note —Primary and secondary is given to the distributor in two forms in percentage & in quantity purchase.</u>

It will be more cleared by studying a heard copy of the invoice.

In market place the scheme can be given like

12+1 (free)

15+1 (free)

Scratch card scheme

How to be calculating the free quantity percentage we should also study.

18. What is the meaning of retailor & wholesaler?

Retailor-retailer typically buys goods from the distributor or wholesaler and then resells them to the public.

Wholesaler-a wholesaler is a person whose business is buying large quantities of goods and selling them is smaller shopkeeper.

The difference between retailers and wholesaler is that while retailers sell direct to consumers, wholesaler sell their goods to small retailors.

19. How to calculate return on investment (ROI)

A ROI man's that whatever amount of money we have investment in the business. What we are getting in return in the form of profit what we call the return on investment (ROI).

A. ROI can be calculating with one company if the distributor is working with one organization only.
B. ROI can be calculated with more than one company if the distributor is working with then one organization.

We have to study four to five practical examples to make it more clear.

Formula for calculating ROI is-

ROI=Gross profit-expenses/total investment *100

Retail Price calculation=MRP/100+Margin of retailor*100

<u>It will be more clear by solving four to five practical examples.</u>

20. What is the company Hierarchy

Company hierarchy in sales-

MD/BD (Managing Director/Board of Director

CEO/MD (Chef Executive Officer/Marketing Director)

Director

Co-Director

President

Vice President

GM (General Manager)

ZSM/RSM (Zone Sales Manager/Regional Manager)

ASM (Area Sales Manager)

SO/TSO (Sales Officer/Territory Sales Officer)

JSO/ASO (junior sales officer/Assistant Sales Officer)

TSI/SE (Territory Sales In charge/Sales Executive)

SR/ISR/PSR (Sales Representative/Interim Sales Representative/ Pilot sales Representative)

21. What sales Person Does before going to the market place for selling a products?

Before going to the market for selling a product it is must to the presales preparation if he is working with retail network.

a. Visiting the distributor.
b. First you will take Stock Position
c. You will check beat plan properly
d. You will check the previous bills supplied or not while doing his last visit in that market.
e. You will check the POP if laying in the distributor go down, you should keep it safely & required POP you should carry in the market
f. You should keep the product sample in your duty beg.
g. You should carry the stationary like stapler/cello tape /FEVICOL etc.

After doing the market in the evening you will came to the distributor point, you will compile all the SKUs and deduct the order stock from the stock which you has taken in the morning & will prepare the short SKU order & will collect the DD/Cheque/take commitment for NEFT for the order which he has written.

<u>Five to six case studies has to be done through mock calls</u>

Date wise Sales dairy Entry is must in the dairy entry the sales person has to write (Town/Distributor/sale/stock/order/claim/any issue which the distributor is having).

<u>After doing the market work what the next work what the sales person do....</u>

So the next working is compiling of order which he has booked from the market. Then what the stock you have taken in the morning he will deduct from the stock these orders what shortage of stock you will make primary order

22. How to use different type sales dairy technical or non-technical-

Prepared though Practically/mock call /case study

23. Personality development

A sales person should look like glittering star in the market.

A. Properly well dressed.
B. Well-polished shoes
C. Well shaved
D. No use of tobacco/gutakha/cigarettes in the market place or distributor place.
E. You should be soft spoken
F. Don't discourse worthless discussion.

For technical sales professional –

For technical professionals. Who are dealing with mobile/motor vehicles/machineries etc. they should keep the following step for their presale preparation.

a. You should have the basic technical knowledge about the product.

b. You should know how to demonstrate the product in working style.

c. You should be well aware about the guaranty & warranty.

d. You should know if any defect comes in the products so where are the service station or showroom so that they can change or repair the product.

e. Paper required for the monthly review meeting.

Monthly review meeting-This is very import part of sales A monthly meeting review is an opportunity to reflect on all your accomplishment and then re adjust your long term goal.

a. Monthly stock & sales statement (Db. wise)

b. Tour plan & forecast For the next month

c. Total area reporting

d. Reporting will be done daily basic/weekly/fortnightly/monthly/ depend upon company rules or requirement.

e. Paid-up stock-paid up stock is that stock which the distributor purchased by doing payments--How to learn the language of sales

The sales person that possesses the most flexibility of behaviour will always control the market.

Sales is one of the key of business success

Sales Force-the people in a company sale goods and service are called its sales force

Lead-a lead is person or business has been identified as a possible customer.

Prospect-a prospect is a lead has been shown strong interest in a product or service.

Qualify-a lead that become a prospect is qualify

To close a sale-a sales person close a sale when he convinces a customer to actually buy a products or service. Closing a sale may involve signing a contract or collect money.

26. How to be a good personality of sales.

What makes a good sales person?

1. Empathy. A good sales person know how to feel their customer feel.
2. Confidence. Believing in the products or service they are selling make good sales person.
3. Honesty. The folks that are best at selling stuff are also honest
4. Product knowledge-An exceptional sales person always start with knowledge. They knowledgeable, down to every detail. On the product they sell, they are expert on product uses.
5. Passionate. When a sales person believes in what they selling, it is more exciting for them to sell.it gives them opportunities to show of a product they are proud to be involved.
6. Organized. The more organized a sales person is with customer information, the more notes they take on what products have been sold.
7. Hungry. Great sales person not only nurture the customer but

they seek and hunger to develop new customer and find to new way to explore more business with existing customer.

8. **Heard working.** Extraordinary sales person understand the sales doesn't stop at the closing of the deal. The sales continue as long as the customer using their service. Great sales person understand there will be complication and that it is up to them, as the customer point to get customer issue resolve in as quickly As soon as possible.

9. **Self-motivated.** Extraordinary sales person recognize the need for support and guidance, however they do not need appreciate feeling babysat. They are self – motivated and take responsibility for their territory.

10. **Time awareness.** Good sales person view time as their most important reputation building commodity. Good sales person to be on time for customer meeting. Because time is the very important part of our life so don't best worthless time.

11. **Work life balance.** Because sales can be an all-consuming 24*7.the best sales person make sure to live with a healthy work life balance

12. **Presale preparation.** <u>What a sales person does before doing a sales call.</u>

The preparation which a sales person does before going to the market is called the presale preparation

This is **very important step doing the sales**

<u>The sales person should keep in mind the following points before going to the market.</u>

a. he should check the beat plan

b. He should check the order or bills supplied or not during his last visit in the same beat

c. He should have the current stock position SKU wise in his dairy

d. He should have the product sample in his beg.

e. He should have carry with POP or dangler, for using any poster or dangler on the outlet the <u>sales person take permission from the shop keeper.</u>

f. Day wise sales Dairy entry.

This is very important for a sales person to make day wise /date wise dairy entry.

In this follow points are to be noted

a. Town
b. Distributor name
c. Stock position
d. Order taken latter head
e. Claim prepared
f. any old issue
g. All beat in covering the distributor.

Reporting can be done on-

A. Daily Basic
B. Weekly basic
C. Forthrightly basic
D. Monthly basic

<u>Format is given you accordingly please understanding.</u>

27. Case Study

Here we have three Type of case study

a. General Products
b. Case Study About Mobile
c. Case Study For Automobile like Car and bikes

Case Study (GP01)

This Company is one of the most reputed origination in India & Dealing in general products like Space Hair Oil & Cosmetic Items. The products qualitative & recognize by some buty exports. The company is going to introduce its products in north India; they are the leader in south India so as sales professional you are going to lunch these products in the market .So do a call to the retailer dealing in general market items.

Before doing the sales Call what information a sales person require.

The following are the information a sales person needs before doing the sales call.

a. physical products
b. Basic Background Company & its owner.
c. Basic ingredients of the products which have been used for making it.
d. Function of every ingredients.
e. MRP/PRICE /RETAIL & WHOLESALE MARGIN /SCHEME
f. Advantage over the competitor.
g. Company Support (media advertisement/display scheme)

h.   Service & availability.

<u>Will Make the Rest of the information practically.</u>

1. Resume Drafting
2. Preparation for the interview
3. Project report of field working
4. Reporting
5. Prepare tour plan
6. How to handling new area
7. How to find out new rural town
8. Making Secondary Scheme (local Level)
9. How to sit
10. How to dress up
11. Primary scheme
12. Scheme calculation
13. Total area report
14. Some General formula has to drafted
15. Monthly sales & sales statement
16. Some Part of communication Skill
17. Some part of Personality development
18. How to calculate retail & whole sale price
19. What step are require find out new distributor
20. How to handling different type of customer.

END.

Contents

Foreword

1. **Basic Meaning of Sales & Marketing**

   Marketing is the macro concept which includes.

a. **Sales**
b. **Banking**
c. **Finance**
d. **Insurance**
e. **Adverting**

   But here we want to become the sales professional so we have to study only about the sales.

   SALES. The basic meaning of sales is the exchange of goods in term of money for earning profit is called sales.

1. **Categories of sales**

   Sales are Categorise in two parts.

a. Direct Sales
b. Indirect Sales

   DIRECT SALES. Direct sales means goods are sold to the direct user/consumer.e.g like vegetable seller; we have seen some gentlemen selling electronic goods door to door. This we call direct sale.

   INDIRECT SALE. Indirect sales men's the goods doesn't sale directly to the user rather it goes through different channels of distribution.

Question arises what are the channels of distribution.
CHANELS OF DISTRIBUTION.

a. FACTORY
b. Depot/warehouse
c. Super stockist
d. Distributors /Stockiest
e. Retailor /wholesaler
f. Users/consumers

Preface

FACTORY. Factory is defined as where the goods are manufactured for the use of consumers.

DEPOT/WAREHOUSE. Depot or warehouse is the place where the factory goods are stoked in bulk quantity for supply to next channel for distribution, the person who runs the operation of the depot is called the carrying & forwarding agents (C&F)

SUPER STOCKIST. Super stockist is the part of distribution that purchases goods from the C&F & supply to the distribution.

DISTRIBUTORS/STOCKIST. Distributor is that part of distribution channel that purchase goods from the super stockist & supply to the retailers /wholesalers

USERS/CONSUMERS. Users/Consumers directly purchase goods

1. **What a Sales Person Sales (Products)**

   A Sales Person requiresthe given information

a. Basic knowledge about the product.
b. If the products are electronic the he should have the technical knowledge about the product.
c. He should have the knowledge how to demonstrate the product in working style.
d. If he is selling the food products he should have the knowledge about the ingredients available in the product & how they are beneficial for the health
e. He should have the knowledge about MRP/Price /Margin

f. **What is a product?**

What a sales person sales. A sales person sale anything that We call it a product.

Acknowledgements

1. **What are types of products?**

   Two types of products.

   a. Consumer products
   b. Technical products
   c. **Consumer products.** Consumergoods are those which satisfy the consumer needs after direct use. Selling those

   Goods the sales person should have the knowledge about
   The basic ingredients of the products MRP rate and margin.

3. **Technical products.** For selling these products the sales person requires the technical knowledge for selling these products e.g. mobile car bikes, electronic machines etc.
4. **What are the sales step required for the selling a products**

   Full knowledge required for selling a products, basic/ technical
   Source/ingredients MRP margin scheme distributor margin and
   Retail margin etc. required for selling a products.

5. **Detailed Explanation of sales step through (ODPEC)**

with

Case studies.

How the sales person dose sales, what are steps required while

Selling a products

O-opening the call

D-Developing the Call

P-Proposing

E-Eliminating the doubts

C-Closing

Opening the Calls-When the sales person visit to a retailor/

Distributor the following step to follow

a. Wishing (good morning,Namaste,Hello)
b. Your name from which company you are.

Developing call-In this step the sales person should develop

The platform between the buyer & seller (relation building &

Prologue

Personal bounding) e.g. whether, politics, local issues, so that

You can build a good relationship with him.

Proposing-In the third step of selling the sales person should

Propose about the product what he is selling.

1. Product's introduction

2. Products Range Show

3. Rates & Scheme

Eliminating the doubts-This is very important step of selling

In this step of selling the sales person should clear all the

Doubts/questions of the buyer (about product wait/ net rate

QPS objection/profits/specialty of products what you sale)

If he is selling technical products he should clear about

Service places & how much time it will take to get repair or

Replace.

Closing- In the last step of selling is order taking. The sales

Person should take maximum order as much as possible, the

Call should be closed in win win situation. Take maximum

Order QTY (the buyer & seller should be happy)

1. **Definition of Customer.** Any people who consume our

product for satisfying his need or requirement is called the consumer.

2. **Types of customer.**
3. Customers are classified in different categories.
4. Calculative Customer
5. Egoistic Customer
6. Talkative Customer
7. Technical Customer
8. Loyal Customer
9. Educated Customer
10. Negligent Customer

Calculative Customer- this type of customer are very calculative & profit conscious, so as a sales person you should be very alert & strong in data figures while doing the call.

CHAPTER ONE

Structural Function of a company's product from company to the consumer.

What are the stage though which the product reaches from company to consumers?

COMPANY/INDUSTRY

DEPOT/WAREHOUSE

SUPERSTOCKIST

DISTRIBUTOR

RETAILOR/WHOLESELLER

CONSUMERS

1. **Terms we are using in sales.**

a. Call-visiting shop for taking order
b. TC-total call-how many shop sales person visit
c. PC/EC Productive Calls/Effective Calls-no of shop given order
d. Outlet /Counter-every shop we call the outlet/counter
e. Throughput/average-Average no of product we are given.
f. Beat-50-60 outlet in market we call it as beat.
g. Rout-rout can be cleared through mock call
h. Frequency-sales person covering the beat, it might be weekly forth nightly (after 15 days and monthly
a. DB(Distributor)
j. Primary Sales-billed to direct company /super

k.   Secondary Sales-you sold the goods in the market
ax.   SKU (Stock Keeping Unit)
all.   4P(Product Price Place Promotion)
n.   AIDA(awareness interest desire action)
o.   ABC (Always be Closing)
p.   ABM (account based marketing)
q.   ABS (account base Selling)
r.   APS (average selling Price)
s.   CRM (customer relationship management)

CHAPTER TWO

How to appoint a new distributor.

For appointment of new distributor in the town we have to go through the follow steps.

The sales person has to do the wholesale market survey at least 25 shops and ask question about their service, behaviour and availability of stocks at distributor.

We have to do the retail survey at least 30 -35 shops their visit frequency and service

After doing the survey we have to prepare the territorial rank of the distributor.

<u>**Question which we have to ask the retailor /wholesaler while doing the market survey**</u>

a. How many distributor come on your shop, (write their name and phone number)
b. Which is the best among all(best men's timely service, good behaviour and proper scheme he is given)

<u>**After doing the market survey we have to meet the shortlisted distributor. Now what question you have to ask to the distributor while appointing.**</u>

a. Self intro and Company intro
b. How many companies you are having distribution & which beats you are covering.

c. How many sales staff you are having for order booking , how many vehicles you are having for market supply.
d. How many outlets you are covering in the town.
e. How many credit you are given in the market
f. You have to ask the question regarding company wise turnover.

CHAPTER THREE

Egoistic Customer- These customers are very conscious about their respect, reputation, image, good will, so as a sales person you should pay proper respect boost-up his ego, goodwill and image

Loyal Customer- This type of customer is very honest & loyal, so as a sales person you should be straight forward with this type of customer.

Talkative Customer- This type of costumer is talkative and interested worthless discussion, so the sales person should be alert not to involve in worthless discussion, you should hold is discussion and come on motive.

Technical Customer- This type of customer are knowledgeable technically about the product. So as a sales person you should have the proper technically knowledge about the product. If some micro technically is out of knowledge then the sales person should say I don't have any idea about it.it I will discuss with my specialist.

Educated Customer- This type of customer is educated and the sales person should do a call with limited discussion. You should answer only the asked question

Negligent Customer- This type of customer are negligent so the sales person should be very alert while taking order, he should check all the stocks properly in his shop while taking order of his product.(no pressure sale)

<u>**For handling these type of customer we have to do case study though mock calls**</u>.

1. Basic meaning of company/industries

A company is a association of person in which the group of people invest their capital for starting their business for earning profit, but an industry is a group of company that involve in one or more business.

CHAPTER FOUR